Pearl

DEBBY ATWELL

HOUGHTON MIFFLIN COMPANY BOSTON 2001

Walter Lorraine Books

Walter Lorraine (wr)Books
Copyright © 2001 by Debby Atwell

All rights reserved. For information about permission
to reproduce selections from this book, write to Permissions,
Houghton Mifflin Company, 215 Park Avenue South,
New York, New York 10003.

Library of Congress Cataloging-in-Publication Data

Atwell, Debby.
    Pearl / by Debby Atwell.
        p. cm.
    Summary: Events in the history of the United States,
from George Washington's presidency through the beginning
of the space program, are related to the experiences of one family.
    ISBN 0-395-88416-0
    [1. United States — History — Fiction. 2. Family life — Fiction.] I. Title.

PZ7 .A8935 Pe 2001
[Fic]—dc21   00-035110
                                                              CIP
                                                              AC

BVG 10 9 8 7 6 5 4 3 2 1

For Mom

This book was inspired by a story told by
American historian Richard Shenkman,
author of *Presidential Ambition*.

At night, when the house is quiet, I look out my bedroom window and see only stars above the dark trees. It's then that I remember family events all the way back to when this country began.

My grandfather told me that when he was just a small boy, he rode in a big parade with the first president of the United States. It was down Wall Street, New York City, on Inauguration Day. Grandfather said George Washington scooped him up just like that out of the crowd and carried him on his horse while everybody cheered. He felt that he was the luckiest person alive.

Father explained to me that everybody felt that way in those days because America was young and anything was possible.

Mother and Father had a farm and, among other things, raised nine children. I was the last. I don't remember my oldest brother, "Texas Dan," ever being at home. He left on a wagon train right after I was born. Folks were going west to find trees full of bluebirds and hills full of gold and such.

Whenever I was frettin' over something, Mother would say, "Pearl, did I ever tell you about the day Dan left for Texas?" I always pretended I had never heard the story, so she'd tell me all over again.

She would say, "The first snow of winter was fallin' as Dan was waving us good-bye. I was smilin' best I could, but I was all a-frettin' inside. I remember hearing geese honkin' their good-bye, too. Made me sad through and through."

At this part of the story, my mother would always give a sigh for dramatic effect. I could just about hear those lonesome geese and feel that lonesome snow.

Then she'd put her arm around me and continue, "But your dear Papa put his arm around me and said, 'Dan's gonna be all right, just like those geese are gonna be.' And Pearl, he was right. Dan was."

Then Mama would say, "And you're gonna be all right too, Pearl."

I always felt better after that.

I can still see my mother and sisters running the farm. All they did was work. Every day, they got up before sunrise and started the fire, heated the kettle, fed the chickens, milked the cows, and dressed me. Then they made the bread, fried the bacon, brewed the coffee, washed the dishes, made the beds, and churned the butter. Then they gathered the wood, plowed the fields, and tended the rows of crops. Then they washed, ironed, sewed, and darned the clothes. I was too young to do anything but be Mother's little Pearlie Pie Face, so she put me up on the cow to keep me out of trouble.

There were no men around. You see, my father and brothers had all gone off to fight in the Civil War to free the slaves.

Abraham Lincoln was president back then. He was a man with black hair and a black beard. We had a picture of him in the parlor. He had a sad and serious face.

When the war was over, only my father came home. John died at Chancellorsville. Henry died at Shiloh. Elliot died at Gettysburg. Only Texas Dan was alive, owing to the fact that he had stayed in Texas, I suppose. I recall that Mother took to grievin' in her room for quite a spell. My sisters, Ruth, Leah, Mary, and Anne, were all gone and married by then, so the house was awful lonesome for me.

A little after that, the railroad finished laying track from Boston to San Francisco. One morning Mother came downstairs in her pretty dress with her hair done. She announced that she and I would be going by train to see Texas Dan. To my surprise, Father let us go.

At the train station, we met a parade of women who wanted to be able to vote. A lady named Susan B. Anthony talked to my mother. My mother told her that women would never be able to vote, but it didn't mean they shouldn't be. Then we got on the train.

Mother and I found Fort Worth, Texas, a mite gamy, with the pigs, dogs, and cattle running about the streets alongside cowboys on horses and such. But we were glad to be off that train.

We'd had a quiet trip out, with an occasional whistle stop followed by a call of "All aboard!" Then clickety-clack, clickety-clack for hours. Like a lullaby it was.

The lullaby stopped outside of Texas, when a herd of buffalo suddenly stampeded around the train. Most of the coaches were knocked off the track. Everything was upside-down in the ditch.

A stagecoach took us into town. Mother was a little shaky. But everything was fine and dandy when she saw her baby boy, my big brother, Texas Dan, again.

After our trip to Texas, I grew fast, but the country grew even faster. Our national heroes back then were folks like Thomas Edison and Thomas Crapper. They invented things like electric lights, telephones, indoor plumbing, and such.

Then one day, I met my hero, David. He thought I was beautiful, which suited me just fine. The next year we married and spent our honeymoon at Niagara Falls, like most newlyweds.

Then we took a train to New York City to see the Statue of Liberty, which France had just given to the United States. It was so beautiful. But I was so daffy with happiness that everything looked beautiful to me back then. Love is right nice but makes you right silly.

They called the nineties gay, I guess because everyone had so much fun. Our daughters, Peg and Emily, were born. I also recall David sold our horses, Charlotte and Brontay, and bought a newfangled machine called an automobile.

Around about then, David's old school chum wired a telegram. It said:

come right away stop see new invention stop Orville

We bundled up the girls and drove the automobile to Kitty Hawk, North Carolina.

On a nippy December morning, we watched Orville fly the first aeroplane. It did not go very far. But I can't forget Orville grinning from ear to ear, and Orville's brother, Wilbur, slapping him on the back. Men. I knew they were happy, but I could see no real purpose to people flying around in the air.

Peg and Emily grew a little every day. Then World War I started in Europe, something about Archduke Ferdinand and a lot of separate treaties. Well, our country kept its promises and went to war. The army hired Wilbur and Orville to design planes to fight battles. I remember thinking how glad I was that I had only daughters, who could not be drafted into the army.

After the war, the country had a ten-year party called the Roaring Twenties. Everybody danced 'the Charleston.' Peg, Emily, and I were able to vote for the first time, too. We helped Warren G. Harding become president of the United States. My girls caused a bit of a stir at the polls with their flapper dresses, bobbed hair, and such. I'll never understand why some people make such a fuss over what young people are wearing. Fancy clothes are just a way of celebrating good times.

fter that, trouble showed up and nobody wore fancy clothes anymore. The Great Depression was what they called it. I remember Will Rogers saying that America was the only country in the world that went to the poorhouse in an automobile.

Most all of the men lost their jobs because the stock market crashed. I never understood what that meant. All I understood was it was mighty tough to keep food on the table.

Peg and Emily were both married by then. They volunteered at the soup kitchen all day on Saturdays, even though their own husbands, Joe and Harry, had jobs.

David and I took our grandsons to the movie theater on those Saturdays, to help our daughters. Moving-picture shows cost ten cents, and that was a lot. But it helped us forget our problems for a while. Joe Jr. and Henry loved those movies. We had our fun somehow. People always do.

olks thought the First World War would be the last war. Never again, we all said. Maybe that's what Hitler was counting on. But one day we woke up and the Nazis were trying to rule the whole world. We had to go to war again.

They were dark times. Peg and Joe moved to Washington, D.C., so Joe could work as a translator. Harry and Emily both worked in an arms factory. Joe Jr. and Henry sailed overseas to fight.

David and I took turns writing letters for the wounded soldiers at the Red Cross hospital. They always started, "Dear Mom and Dad, I'm okay." But it was seldom true.

Henry didn't come home. I finally understood how my mother felt after the Civil War. My heart broke for my daughter.

We dropped the biggest bomb ever made, the first atomic bomb. Then the war was over. There was great joy, followed by great sorrow for all those we'd lost. Myself, I wondered what the atomic bomb meant to the world. It was an awful thing.

Memorial Day became the most important event in our town. We had a big parade, patriotic speeches, a community picnic, and fireworks at night. Mothers like Emily placed flowers on graves. A trumpet played taps.

I first heard about the United Nations in our mayor's speech on one such occasion. He read the opening words to the UN charter: "We the peoples of the United Nations have determined to save succeeding generations from the scourge of war, which twice in our lifetime has brought untold sorrow to mankind."

I could only hope those words would hold true.

We grew older. David got a cane, and I got a hearing aid. Peg wrote from Alabama that her son, Joe Jr., and her daughter-in-law, Ivy, were going to have a baby, and did we want to come down and live with them and help raise our first great-grandchild? We sure did.

When we got to Alabama, David bought the first television on the block. Moving-picture shows in your own home! We met every child in the neighborhood that night. It was wonderful. The children, that is. My recollection of the television was that it was overrated. I've always preferred children to television.

Every Sunday morning I'd awaken to hear the sweetest singing coming from somewhere on Dexter Street, out past the baseball field behind our house. One morning that singing got me right out of bed. I crossed the baseball field and found the music.

I was standing in the back of a church, pretty tired from the walk and looking for a place to sit down, when a little girl in a white dress came up from behind and took me by the hand. She said she saw me coming across the field and that I could share a seat with her. Then she led me right up front. I was just in time to hear the Reverend Martin Luther King Jr. preach about the civil rights of all American people.

Last month we had a party on David's and my wedding anniversary. Emily and her family flew down from Rockland, Maine. Folks from all sides of the family arrived. What a wonderful time we had. And the best thing was to hold my second great-granddaughter, Pearl! I could have watched her sleeping all day just like that, but suddenly everyone sat down to watch TV. We saw a rocket lift off. Everybody counted THREE . . . TWO . . . ONE . . . BLAST-OFF! Then they cheered. The noise woke Pearl, and she gave me a great big smile. Like it was all for her.

Call me balmy, but I was struck with a notion. I was sure that one day the family would see little Pearl ride in a spaceship and walk on the moon.

I could almost hear Father say, "Pearl, you can dream like that because the United States is young and anything is possible."

I think that must be true, because I could see that little Pearl had my father's sky-blue eyes.

1789
Pearl's grandfather rides with Washington on Inauguration Day.

1850s
Westward expansion. Dan leaves in 1858.

1861
The Civil War begins.

1862
Pearl is born.

1865
The Civil War ends. Pearl is three.

1869
The Railroad crosses the United States. Pearl is seven.

1885
Pearl and David visit the Statue of Liberty on their honeymoon. Pearl is twenty-three.

1903
The Wright Brothers fly at Kitty Hawk. Pearl is forty-one. Emily is six. Peg is three.

1917
America enters World War I.

1921
Women get the vote. Pearl is fifty-nine. Peg marries and has a son in 1926. Emily has a son in 1927.

1930s
The Great Depression. Pearl is in her sixties.

1945
World War II ends. Emily's son dies in battle. Pearl is eighty-three.

1954
Pearl and David move to Alabama. Pearl is ninety-two.

1955
Pearl hears Martin Luther King preach. Pearl is ninety-three.

1960
Pearl and David's seventy-fifth anniversary. The space age begins.